LOCKED OUT

GUARDING SECRETS

LOCKED OUT

GUARDING SECRETS

PATRICK JONES

darbycreek

MINNEAPOLIS

Darby Creek
A division of Lerner Publishing Group, Inc.
241 First Avenue North
Minneapolis, MN 55401 USA

For reading levels and more information, look up this title at
www.lernerbooks.com.

The images in this book are used with the permission of: © Pashok/
Dreamstime.com (young woman); © iStockphoto.com/DaydreamsGirl (stone);
© Maxriesgo/Dreamstime.com (prison wall) © Clearviewstock/Dreamstime.
com, (prison cell).

Main body text set in Janson Text LT Std 12/17.5.
Typeface provided by Adobe Systems.

Library of Congress Cataloging-in-Publication Data

Jones, Patrick, 1961–
    Guarding secrets / by Patrick Jones.
        pages   cm. — (Locked out)
    Summary: Since her mother went to prison to await execution,
eleventh-grader Camila Hernandez has been shuffled from one aunt to
another, avoiding friendships and keeping to herself in hopes no one will
learn her secret, and worrying that she will turn out to be a criminal, too.
    ISBN 978-1-4677-5801-7 (lib. bdg. : alk. paper)
    ISBN 978-1-4677-6185-7 (EB pdf)
    [1. Interpersonal relations—Fiction. 2. Secrets—Fiction. 3. Conduct
of life—Fiction. 4. Aunts—Fiction. 5. Prisoners' families—Fiction.
6. Dating (Social customs)—Fiction. 7. Hispanic Americans—Fiction.
8. Anaheim (Calif.)—Fiction.] I. Title.
PZ7.J7242Gu 2015
[Fic]—dc23   2014018697

Manufactured in the United States of America
1 – SB – 12/31/14

To Gretchen Wronka, who guarded my
back for so many years.

1

"Do you want to know a secret?"

Someone was whispering behind Camila. She took her eyes off the row of long black dresses in front of her to dart a glance at the two girls behind her. She recognized both of them. She prayed they didn't recognize her.

They were from her current school, juniors like her. Lisa Guevara or Herrera, and Angela, or Angelina, or something like that. Camila got the sense that they were both divas. Too much makeup, perfume, and attitude. They probably didn't know Camila's name, let alone her secret.

"I heard Ricky likes. . . ." And with that, Camila tuned out the girls' voices. Rattling on about stupid crushes, acting like each break-up and hook-up was a matter of life or death. If they only knew.

In the corner of the store, a young black security guard stared at Camila like she was a cockroach on a white rug. The watchful store clerks were giving her the same look.

She started shuffling through the marked-down dresses faster, until she found one in her size. She checked the tag: still pricey, even on discount. This was why she shopped so rarely, and almost never at the mall. Like all the relatives she'd lived with over the past decade, Camila's aunt Maria worked hard but never had extra money to buy nice clothes.

Behind her, she heard one of the girls—Lisa—ask, "Hey, don't you go to Anaheim High?"

Camila didn't turn around, not even when the girl tapped her on the back, sending a shock through her system. "You deaf or something?" Lisa demanded.

Camila pulled in a deep breath, tugged down on the long sleeves of her oversized black hoodie, and pivoted. Eyes down, she stared at the girls' identical black four-inch heels.

"I know you," Lisa said. "We're in advisory together. Camila Hernandez, right?"

A nod served as Camila's only answer.

"What's the dress for?" asked the other girl. Camila didn't respond. Instead she looked past the girls at the security guard.

Lisa snapped her gum. "That's way too boring for homecoming."

Camila fought an urge to laugh. Her, go to the school homecoming dance—right. This dress was for—well, it *was* for a homecoming of sorts, her mom's after so many years away.

Without a word to the girls, Camila headed for a dressing room. Inside the stall, she ripped the price tag and sensor strip from the dress, then stuffed it under her hoodie.

A few minutes later she walked casually toward the store's exit, past the two girls—who were still watching her—past the other customers, past the security guard. No alarm went off.

No shouts followed her. If Lisa and what's-her-face had guessed her game, they hadn't bothered to tell the guard. At least not fast enough. In another moment Camila had blended into the crowd of passing shoppers.

As she made her way toward the mall exit near the bus stop, she couldn't stop thinking about all the answers she could've given those girls. Did they want to know a secret? Well, Camila had one she'd kept most of her life, walking around with it like a sharp stone in her black high-tops.

She boarded the bus with the question still on her mind. *What's the dress for?* Her answer was simple and sad. It was for her mother's funeral.

2

"Where have you been?" Aunt Maria asked as soon as Camila walked in the door.

"Out," Camila muttered as she made her way toward her bedroom. The apartment was tiny. As she moved from relative to relative, it seemed her world got smaller.

Her aunt followed her. "Out where?"

"Just at the mall." She could've lied to her aunt, since not telling the truth ran in her family. Aunt Maria and other relatives had lied to her for years. *Your mother went to Mexico to care for her father* was the story she was told.

A noble tale of family sacrifice.

"You're supposed to come home right after school—" Aunt Maria started as Camila reached her room.

Camila slammed the door to shut out the lecture. She'd had enough of those back when she lived with Aunt Rosa. The past year that she'd been with Aunt Maria had been fairly quiet, fairly drama-free, by comparison. But Maria still got high and mighty on her sometimes, and Camila wasn't in the mood.

She stashed the stolen dress in her closet, flopped onto her bed, and turned on the radio. Unlike most kids, Camila's didn't have a phone. Partly because of money, but partly by choice. She liked to keep her life private. To live in her dreams and shut out the rest of the world.

Deep into the booming music, Camila was jarred by a loud banging on her door.

"You have a visitor!" Aunt Maria yelled.

Camila turned down the music. "Who?" she called. The split second it took her aunt to answer felt like forever. There were only two names she wanted to hear, and one—her mother's—

was impossible.

"That boy."

"Be right out!" Camila vaulted from her bed to the dresser. As she checked herself in the mirror, she glanced at the photo of her mother that sat next to it. Not a recent one—it was from her mom's high school years. Before years of drugs and violence had hardened her mom's features. Before the gang tattoos of Los Reyes de Aztlán had filled her mom's arms.

After brushing her long, thick hair and applying a fresh coat of lip gloss, Camila started for the door. Then she doubled back, this time heading to her closet. She quickly swapped her black hoodie for a bright green blouse. She usually wore black, but green seemed right for Juan. After another glance in the mirror, she left her room.

"He's out front," said Aunt Maria.

"You didn't let him come up?" Camila shot her a dark look. *If she starts in about men being trouble, like Aunt Rosa used to do . . .*

"I offered. He said he was fine waiting outside."

Which was where Camila found him a

minute later, out on the cracked sidewalk in front of the apartment building. In the street, she saw his black pickup.

"Hey, Camila," Juan said softly. Camila could barely hear him over the soundtrack of the neighborhood—planes overhead, bass booming from cars on the streets, and sirens in the background. He kissed her cheek. "You look nice."

"Thanks, you too." Juan always dressed up like he was going to church. Clean shaven with short hair, he looked like the marine he hoped to one day become. They'd known each other nine months, and had been dating for almost six, but Camila still felt a little catch in her throat whenever she saw him.

"So I was heading home from an Honor Society meeting and thought I'd swing by," he said. "Wanna go somewhere?"

By "somewhere" he probably meant anywhere outside this neighborhood. Juan's family lived in a safe part of town, no kids selling drugs out in the open, no fights breaking out on a daily basis. She knew Juan's dad didn't like him spending time over here. She guessed he thought like many people did: *If you come from the hood, you are one.*

"Sure," she said. "Somewhere with air conditioning?"

"I know the perfect coffee place," said Juan. He didn't suggest going to his own home. By now he'd probably sensed that Camila wasn't comfortable there. Someone else was always around—Juan's dad, mom, sisters—looking at her like she was a puzzle that didn't deserve to be solved.

She felt that way enough without the Cruz family rubbing it in.

So many times when she glanced in a mirror, she was reminded of how much she looked like her mom at that age. Some days she stared at her mom's high school photo, amazed at the resemblance, loving it. Other days, she couldn't stand to look at it. If she shared an outside, maybe she shared the inside.

She couldn't bear the thought of Juan—or Juan's family, or anyone—looking at her closely enough to find out.

3

"Who would like to lead us in prayer?" Father Gomez, doddering but kind, looked expectantly at the members of his youth group. As usual, when no one volunteered, Juan took the lead.

Camila tried to concentrate, but it was hard. Not just because she was standing next to Juan, close enough that their shoulders brushed. She didn't really like the youth group. Aunt Maria had insisted she join. *It'll be good for you—give you something constructive to do.* "Constructive," in Aunt Maria's vocabulary, basically meant anything that wasn't illegal. Aunt Rosa had told enough stories from Camila's wild days to put Maria on constant yellow alert. She was always asking Camila what she was up to, who she was hanging out with, who her friends were.

Friends—as if she had any, besides Juan. Outside of school, where she disappeared easily, the youth group was her only point of contact with people her age. She knew she wasn't smart enough to hang out with the good students, not dangerous enough for the bad ones, not social enough for the popular ones, and not an artist or an athlete. She guessed that few students knew her name. Which was just the way she wanted it.

Really, the only good thing about the youth group was that she'd met Juan here. At first she'd resisted his efforts to get to know her, his offers to hang out. But Juan was persistent and polite. And as she learned more about him, the more she liked him. He was sweet and smart. Responsible. Safe.

After the prayer, Father Gomez said, "The theme for tonight is forgiveness. We talk a lot about the importance of forgiving our enemies, but I want to focus on something that's often harder: forgiving those we're close to. The people we love—friends, family—can let us down, can even betray us. Those are the wounds that cut deepest and take longest to heal. Would anyone like to share an example . . ."

That was all Camila heard before she bolted from her seat.

The next thing she knew she was standing outside the building. She wished for a cigarette or a joint like those she'd smoked when she lived with Aunt Rosa in Riverside.

"You OK?" It was Juan. He put his arms around her, pulling her close to his six-foot frame.

"Sorry, just sometimes . . ." Camila stopped. The less said the better.

Juan said, "You can talk to me about it, you know. Whatever it is that's bothering you."

"No, it's fine. Really. I'm fine. Forget about it."

"OK. If you say so." Juan pulled her tighter as a cooling fall twilight descended. One thing she'd quickly come to love about Juan: he never pushed her. He let her have her secrets.

"Shame you can't come on Saturday," Juan

said. Camila felt herself shriveling a bit. It was his sister Marcela's quinceañera celebration. Camila was a little jealous—she hadn't had one of her own, when she'd been living with Aunt Rosa. But that wasn't why she'd refused the invitation. She couldn't tell him the real reason. Not now, not ever.

Family obligations, she'd said when he invited her. Not really a lie.

"But I understand," Juan said. "My dad always says the family tree is stronger than any California redwood."

Camila pulled Juan close to her. *No, you can't and never will understand anything about my family. My family tree doesn't have roots. It has metal bars and steel doors.*

4

SEPTEMBER 27 / SUNDAY / EARLY MORNING / ANAHEIM BUS STATION

Five a.m., still full dark. Camila had never been a morning person. But she was completely alert as she and Aunt Maria boarded the prison shuttle bus. She always was on days like these. Through the four-hour trip to Chowchilla, the visit itself, and then the trek back: no sleep, no peace.

As always the bus overflowed with children, most of them younger than Camila. For ten years, she had watched the children get younger as she got older. She donned an LA Angels baseball cap to hide her face, just in case someone from school or church saw her. It didn't matter that if they were on the bus, they were in same situation. There wouldn't be any comfort in that. She wanted this part of her life separate and secret. After today, that would be easy to do. After today, she'd never set foot on this bus again.

"What are you thinking about?" Aunt Maria asked as they sat down.

"I just wonder if I'll miss being on this bus," Camila answered, touching the torn upholstery.

"I won't miss it," said Aunt Maria. "I hate it."

Camila didn't respond. Could you only miss things you loved?

By now, Camila knew every sign along the highway by heart. As a game, she'd guess how long it'd take them to reach certain landmarks. This driver, an older black man, drove faster than some others, but it always seemed to take four hours.

No more than half an hour out of Anaheim, Aunt Maria fell asleep. Camila didn't mind. She was used to making these journeys alone.

Every now and then, there would be a boy her age who tried to hit on her, or a girl who tried to make friends, but Camila wasn't interested. Sometimes she'd play games with some of the younger children. But this time, she kept to herself with the project she'd planned for the journey: rereading a packet full of her mom's letters and handmade cards.

She had a ten year supply to choose from, so she'd taken the ones from Mother's Day and her birthday. They were almost always the longest, yet hard to read because they were stained with tears from the writer and the reader. The words were mostly the same. *Love you, miss you, be good, see you soon, you're my special girl.* Mostly lies. Never any explanations. Those had come from relatives, piece by piece—each piece uglier than the last.

"It's my mom's birthday!" yelled a young girl—maybe seven. But then again, Camila thought all young girls looked about seven, the age she was when she first boarded the bus. Camila smiled at the little girl. It wasn't a real smile, but the girl didn't need to know that.

Aunt Maria woke up at about the halfway point. She and Camila talked about nothing much. Aunt Maria's world was as small as Camila's. She worked, went to church, and then worked some more. It seemed like the life lived by most of the women on their block.

The energy on the bus revved up as the bus exited the highway toward the access road. The children gathered up their things. The parents, grandparents, aunts, uncles, and guardians took a collective deep breath.

"There's my mom's sign!" the little girl yelled at Camila as the bus passed the wire fence and the sign for the women's facility.

Camila almost wished she could share the girl's excitement. *How many times will she take this bus?* Camila wondered. *How many years? I'll bet the day she makes her last visit, she'll be just as happy as she is now, because on that day her mom will be coming home.*

That was why Camila rarely talked to the other kids on the bus. Most of them could imagine a time when their parents would be free again. Unless their parents were serving life without parole. But even those families, Camila thought, had more reason for hope than she did.

Her mom, Gina Hernandez, wasn't sentenced to life, but to death.

5

"When it is our turn?" a young boy behind Camila whined to a young man who looked not much older than Camila. They were new, so they didn't know that the four-hour bus trip to the prison was a joy compared with the endless visitor intake process.

"I can't wait to hug Mommy!" the boy shouted, and Camila felt another tug at her gut. She used to be able to hug her mother—contact visits, they're called—but that was years ago, before her mom shoved a shiv into a guard who "disrespected me," as her mom said. The guard recovered, but Camila's mom had lost what few privileges she'd had.

After the bus stopped and the families stepped out, women on the other side of the doors began leaving their small cells to prepare for their visits. Most of the families headed toward the main visiting area, but Camila, her aunt, and a few others peeled off in a different direction. The new young man and his son went with Camila's group.

"Hurry up and wait," Aunt Maria sighed as she sat on the hard bench. Camila scarfed down the candy bar in her purse, then put the purse in a locker.

"Visitors for Gina Hernandez," the guard said. He almost snarled her mother's name, which Camila understood. If she worked here, she'd never smile either. Camila and her aunt walked toward the first guard station, where the paperwork was inspected. Even though he'd seen it many times, the guard—who was white, like the rest of the prison staff—took his time, asked questions, and made the long wait longer.

"You are the legal guardian of the minor

child?" the guard asked in a monotone.

Aunt Maria nodded, but that wasn't good enough for the guard. He made her say "Yes."

Then he examined their clothing, making sure what they wore fit the many restrictions related to color, style, maybe even fashion sense. Camila wondered if kids at school would be so quick to complain about dress codes and metal detectors if they went through this routine.

"What's in the packet?" the guard barked at Camila.

"Letters." Camila couldn't make eye contact.

"You can only bring in ten documents."

"Camila, you can't take those in," Aunt Maria said. "I have important papers for your mother to sign. I thought I told you."

Camila sighed and returned the packet to the locker. When she returned, she and her aunt were sent to the back of the line to start the whole process over again.

After finally passing through the gatekeeper guard's endless interrogation, they moved to the metal detector. Even though she passed, one of the female guards patted Camila down, as usual.

A few minutes later she found herself sitting in a tiny room with her mom, her aunt, and a white correctional officer. No windows, no light. Small talk first. *How are you, you look good, how's school, how's church, sign these papers . . .* A guard cautiously handed Camila's mom a pen. She signed the papers without reading them. Returned the pen without trying to stab anyone. And then . . .

"Are you going to be there?" Camila's mom asked.

"There" was Folsom Prison, two hours north of here, where the California death chamber was located. "There" was where her mom would be taken in twelve days. "There," unless another judge issued a stay of execution, her mom would be put to death.

"No, Gina," Aunt Maria answered. "It's a Friday. I have work, Camila has school."

"Good." Camila's mother tapped her fingers on the table. "*She'll* be there. Watson's wife." Camila knew the name as well as she knew her mother's: Officer Chandler Watson, the man her mom had killed when she was just twenty-one.

"Have you prayed and asked for the family's forgiveness?" Aunt Maria asked.

"Of course," Camila's mom said. She claimed to have found God, but not until after she had jabbed the shiv into the CO. *Maybe if she'd found God earlier*, Camila thought, *we'd be together in a room filled with light, not in this above-ground dungeon.*

"They'll never be healed until they forgive you," Aunt Maria said.

"Speaking of forgiveness," said Gina. "Camila, I want to ask for yours."

Camila stared, speechless.

"Please, Camila. Please forgive me."

Forgive you? I don't even know you. This was the woman who'd birthed her, who'd written her those loving letters. But she was also the woman who'd committed terrible crimes for Los Reyes.

Camila looked helplessly at Aunt Maria, and for the first time in the hour-long visit, she started to cry. Aunt Maria pulled Camila tight against her. Her mom tried to reach across the table for her, but the guard smacked his thin black baton against the table. "No PC!" he said.

Gina didn't take the hint. Instead, she threw herself over the small table to latch onto her daughter's hands. The CO yelled, but Gina rose, kicked the chair back, and leaned forward to smother Camila in a hug.

Camila couldn't pull away. Didn't want to pull away. Suddenly Gina was her mother again. Not a stranger with blood on her hands. Just her mother who loved her. Camila held her mom so tightly that her knuckles turned white as she locked her hands.

The CO grabbed Gina's arms but couldn't pry them apart. "Let go, now!"

Gina hung on even tighter, both crying and screaming over the CO's yelling. A second guard entered the room and raced toward her mother.

"Camila, as long as you remember me, I'll never die!" Gina shouted as both of the guards pulled at her mother's arms like some game of tug-of-war. The COs locked her mom's hands behind in her in cuffs and dragged her kicking and screaming from the room. Then there was silence, except for the words still echoing in Camila's head: *Forgive me.*

Few passengers cried on the way to the prison. Almost all cried on the way home.

Camila and Aunt Maria sat in silence at first, letting their tears stream unchecked. Then Camila asked, "Is anyone from our family going to be there?"

"I doubt it."

"I'm surprised. I thought Grandma Vickie would be in the front row."

"Don't talk about your grandmother that way."

"She hates Mom. And me."

Aunt Maria didn't argue the point. Camila had lived with practically every member of the Hernandez family in southern California, except her grandmother, whom she'd seen only at rare family reunions. They never spoke. Her grandmother had never hugged her, always looked at her as if Camila were some foul thing.

"What were the papers you had her sign?" Camila asked.

"Legal stuff, a will, those kinds of things."

Camila had thought about becoming a lawyer once—had dreamed of somehow finding a way to get her mom free. But now she hated it all: lawyers, judges, guards, the system.

"She asked her lawyer to stop fighting it, you know," Aunt Maria said. "This is it." There was a thin current of relief in her voice, and Camila didn't blame her for it. She knew Aunt Maria didn't want Gina dead—unlike Grandma Vickie and maybe Aunt Rosa. Maria was just tired.

"Is there anything of your mother's that you want?" Aunt Maria asked.

Camila just shook her head. Her mother had

nothing she wanted. The only thing she craved her mother couldn't give her: she wanted her childhood back.

"She's going to donate her organs," Aunt Maria said. "She wants to do something good."

"Who would want them?" Camila burst out. "They're probably still filled with meth." *If she wanted to do something good*, Camila thought, *she could've let Officer Watson live and stayed out of prison.*

Aunt Maria clasped her hand hard on Camila's leg. "She got clean when she got pregnant with you and stayed clean for a year."

"And then relapsed."

"You don't know the power of addiction, Camila."

Camila had only vague childhood memories of her mother in a meth daze. But she had a much stronger memory of Aunt Rosa catching her coming home high one night. *You're becoming just like your mother, a worthless addict.*

It was what the whole family thought, what everyone who knew about her connection to Gina Hernandez thought. Like mother, like daughter. And for a few years she'd been willing to go down that path. She'd shoplifted, tried alcohol and a few soft drugs, fought back when someone tried to beat her up. But she'd backed away from all of that after the first arrest—after Aunt Rosa had given her that newspaper article. Out of all the hundreds of articles written about Gina Hernandez, that one had been the first Camila had actually read. Every line of newsprint was seared into her memory, deeper than any warning or insult Rosa had thrown at her.

The bus stopped at the same dimly-lit diner it always did. Camila and Aunt Maria filed off the bus with the other passengers. Inside, Camila looked at the menu and tried not to think about how soon her mom would be choosing her last meal. Tried not to think about her mom at all. As usual, she failed.

7

"We wanna talk to you."

The two girls from the mall stood waiting for Camila just outside advisory. She tried to walk past them into the classroom, but one of them stuck out her arm. "Are you freakin' deaf, Camila?"

So, they knew her name. Fine. Done. "Get out of my way."

"I'm Lisa and this is Angela," said Lisa, the mouthier one.

"I don't care." What did they want from her? Everyone always wanted something.

"Look, the other day at the mall, it was

weird," added Angela, the sidekick. "We didn't mean to hassle you."

"Fine. Can I go now?"

"Do you do that often?" Lisa whispered. "You know, lift stuff."

Camila didn't answer. In her wild days back in Riverside, lifting was part of the life. Rosa told her it would land her in the same place as her mother. The one night Camila spent in juvie was enough, but every now and then, if she really needed something—not wanted, but needed something. . . . "Why?"

"I saw this necklace at the—" Lisa started.

"No." Camila didn't do favors and she didn't need any. Favors led to connections, and connections led to questions, and questions led her no place she wanted to go.

She pushed her way past the two girls, but Lisa grabbed her arm. "Hey, no, it's cool. I just wondered, that's all. We asked around about you . . ."

Camila's blood froze. "And?"

"And nothing," Angela said. "Where'd you go to school before?"

"None of your business," Camila said.

"What is wrong with you?" Lisa shot back. "I mean, we're trying to be nice."

Nice—she'd met nice people before. Been betrayed by nice people before. It was never worth the risk.

"She's freakin' paranoid," Angela muttered to Lisa as the bell rang. Other students pushed past the girls into the classroom.

"Girls, have a seat!" called the math teacher, Mr. Bell, but none of them moved.

"Don't get in my business," Camila hissed. "Or else."

She waited. If they knew about her mom, they probably would have already said something, but this would be their last chance. Camila held her breath. Once people found out, and somehow they always did, the result was always the same. Half the people shunned her, assuming she was bad news like her mother. The other half embraced her for the very same reason. Camila wanted neither. She just wanted, more than anything, to feel normal.

"Or else what?" Lisa asked Camila. So they didn't know. Yet.

Camila narrowed her eyes to slits and gave them the same cold glare she'd seen her mom use on guards. Without saying a word, she turned and went to her desk.

Juan handed his phone to Camila as soon as they sat down to eat in the cafeteria. "Check out the pictures from the quinceañera." Camila studied the photo on the screen. In it, Juan stood with several relatives, including an older man who could have been his twin, separated by twenty years. "That's my uncle Javier. He's a marine. He's my role model, along with my dad."

"You look a lot alike," Camila said, forcing a smile. "Both handsome." She and Juan scrolled through the rest of the photos, but out of the corner of her eye, Camila watched for Angela and

Lisa. Instead she saw something worse: a skinny kid who looked way too familiar. Camila buried her face in Juan's shoulder to avoid being seen.

"I'm sorry I couldn't be there," she mumbled.

"Well, I do have two other younger sisters, so maybe the next one."

Camila smiled, for real now. So Juan expected them to still be dating in a few more years. Most of her life she'd been shuffled from one relative to the next, never staying anywhere long enough to matter. The idea of a future that she could plan for—a future with Juan in it—made her feel older and younger, stronger and more fragile, all at once. "You're sure that will be OK with your parents?"

Juan put his phone down on the table. "Look, Camila, don't worry about that. It's not that they have anything against you personally. It's just that my dad tends to think the worst about everybody our age, especially people who live in your neighborhood."

"Where you come from doesn't make you a certain way." Even as the words left her lips, she wanted to take them back. She wondered if she'd just lied to earnest and honest Juan.

"I know that," Juan said. "He does too. He's just a tough customer. My mom too."

And as always with Juan, or anyone Camila had gotten the least bit close to, she was at a loss for what to say next. Always fearing she'd need to answer for herself, for her family. *Dad? I don't know because my mom never knew. Mom? Meth-head, gang member, and murderer.*

"Camila, I know you don't like to get involved in school stuff," Juan started. There was a rare nervousness in his voice. "But the homecoming dance is coming up in a few days and I was wondering if—"

"It's not a few days, Juan, it's a week from Friday."

"You must have the date circled on your calendar," Juan joked. "Does that mean—"

"No." She did have the date circled, but not because it was homecoming. "I can't go," she said.

"Why not?"

"Well, for starters, I don't have money to buy a new dress." She paused. Juan said nothing, didn't react at all. "But mostly, it's just not a good time. A lot of family stuff going on, that's all." She flashed what she hoped was a sly grin. "Hope that's not a deal breaker or anything."

"You kidding me? Of course not."

On impulse, Camila kissed Juan full on the lips, which got a reaction from people at a nearby table. She pulled back quickly. She hated calling attention to herself, especially now. The skinny kid she'd noticed a minute ago seemed to be looking around the crowded room for a place to sit.

"Good," she said. "I figured I could count on you still liking me, dance or no dance."

Juan pulled Camila close, burying his head against her neck, resting his lips against her right ear. "I don't like you, Camila," Juan whispered. "I think I love you."

Love—that was a word she'd heard a million times, and what did she have to show for it? What was love, other than shorthand for broken promises?

She closed her eyes and held her breath so she wouldn't admit the truth: *I love you too.*

9

"Didn't you used to go to Sierra Middle School?"

Camila looked up at the person standing in front of her locker. It was the skinny guy from lunch. She remembered him, not fondly, but that was true of most of her school experiences. Riverside, Corona, Long Beach, several schools in the Los Angeles district—all places she'd rather forget. Her time at Sierra had been brief for the usual reason. One family member had gotten sick of her and pawned her off on another.

"No," she lied.

Camila closed her locker and started to walk down the hall, but he followed her. "I know you. You're that chick whose mom—"

Camila whirled on him. "Listen, you don't know me. Understand?"

"Nah, girl, I remember you. Killer Camila." He grinned. A shiver snaked up Camila's spine.

She kept walking, hoping to lose him in the end-of-the-day chaos of the hallways.

The guy darted in front of her to block her path. "What's the big deal? Everybody at Sierra gots somebody inside. I mean, my pop's doing a dime at San Quentin. It ain't nothing."

Camila stared at the floor. It looked as if it hadn't been waxed in years.

"Look—Steven, right?" The kid nodded. Camila wasn't sure how she remembered his name, but was glad she did. It made this just a fraction easier. "It's different for girls."

"What are you talking about?"

"Think of all the people in prison. How many of them are women? And how many of *them* are . . ." She didn't say the last three syllables. "I mean, it was a huge deal when she got sentenced. In the news and everything. Because she's a woman."

"Shot a cop right in the face," Steven said. And laughed, way too loud. "Man, I'd like to meet her. Shake her hand, thank her for that."

Camila thought about saying, *Then you'd better hurry, she's only got eleven more days.* But then again, maybe he knew that somehow. Maybe he knew everything, and maybe he'd tell everyone.

"Look, people here don't know. I want to keep it that way."

She skirted past him and headed for the front doors, but Steven followed her.

"So what's the scene here?" he asked, like he was making casual conversation. "Whose turf?"

"I don't know."

They were almost at the front doors. Camila thought about running the rest of the way but decided not to. It might draw attention.

"What's your problem?" Steven snapped.

Camila turned. "Just leave me alone, OK?" She fixed Steven with a hard stare, just like she'd used on Lisa and Angela.

Except Steven didn't blink. He stared back

with cold brown eyes. Hearing the buses outside revving their engines, Camila reached for the door. Steven reached forward too, but not for the door. He grabbed her right arm and pulled her sleeve up.

"What are you doing?"

Steven stared at Camila's bare right arm. "Just wondering, you know."

"Wondering what?" She yanked her arm away and pulled her sleeve down.

Steven lifted the sleeve of his jacket. "In my family, it's like father, like son."

Camila started running then. She ran all the way to the bus. But she couldn't outrun the image burned into her brain: the Los Reyes tattoo covering Steven's right arm.

10

"So, Camila, what are your plans?"

Camila sat in the backseat of Juan's dad's car waiting for Juan, who had run back inside the activity center to confer with Father Gomez. Usually Camila took the bus to and from youth group, so that Juan wouldn't have to drive in her neighborhood. But tonight Juan's father was picking Juan up for a family event, and he'd offered to take Camila home too. Now she was trapped in the car with him.

"My plans?" she echoed. *What does he really want to know?* Camila wondered. *My plans after*

40

high school? With your son? For how to deal with my mom being executed by the State of California? "I mean, I'm not really sure. My life's a little up in the air right now . . ."

"Juan plans to join the Marines," Juan's father said proudly. "His uncle and I both served—my brother's still active. To be a marine takes a lot of discipline and self-control. I know my son has these traits, and I expect anyone who spends time with him to share them. Do you understand what I'm saying, Camila?"

His eyes found hers in the rearview mirror. Camila looked away, out the window. What was taking Juan so long? "Yes, sir."

"It's a shame you won't be able to go to homecoming with him. He had his heart set on going."

Camila didn't respond. What did he want from her?

"I understand from Juan that you have some family issues, and that's why you couldn't go to homecoming with him. Is that right? Is it something you want to talk about?"

"I'd rather not get into it, Mr. Cruz." Camila

couldn't believe Juan had told his dad. She'd thought she could trust Juan. Aunt Rosa was always saying, "Men are trouble. They can't be trusted. Trust no one except flesh and blood. If your mother had done that, instead of getting mixed up with lowlifes like Raul Mero . . ." And on and on.

Of course, Juan was nothing like the men Camila's mother had gotten involved with. But maybe the real truth was shorter than Aunt Rosa's message. *Trust no one.*

"I don't mean to pry," Juan's father said, though that seemed to be exactly what he meant to do. "Is there anything we could do to help? Anything that would make it possible for you to go to the dance? Do you need money or...?"

Who does he think I am, Cinderella? Was he asking so many questions because he really wanted to help, or was he just another nosy adult trying to invade her privacy? "No, sir. Thanks, but it's nothing like that."

They sat together in silence. Another adult trick.

"I don't know much about you or your family," Juan's dad said. "Since you and my son seem somewhat serious about each other, I'd like to meet your parents."

Camila took a deep breath before she launched into the standard lie. "I live with my aunt. My parents died in a car accident in Mexico when I was a baby." She'd said it so many times to so many different people that it almost seemed like the truth. "I don't like to talk about it."

"I'm sorry."

On the bright side, he shut up after that and clicked on the radio to a sports station. Camila put in her buds, turned on her music, and waited for Juan. Wondered if she could still trust him. Even though she'd just lied to Juan's father, as she'd lied to so many adults over the years, she wanted to be able to tell Juan the truth. Not now, but one day. Was even that too much to hope for?

As Juan emerged from the activity center with a Bible in his hand, Camila thought about her Bible at home, the one she'd been given at her confirmation. It wasn't the book itself she thought about, but the news article tucked in the pages, next to Psalm 23:4 (*Even though I walk through the darkest valley, I will fear no evil*), that confirmed her worst fears.

11

WOMAN CONVICTED IN MURDER OF LOS ANGELES POLICE OFFICER; WILL FACE DEATH PENALTY

A member of the transnational criminal gang Los Reyes de Aztlán was convicted Wednesday in the murder of a Los Angeles police officer who had responded to a call near LAX.

Prosecutors said Officer Chandler Watson, who had been with the department for less than two years, was fatally shot by Gina Hernandez, age 21. An accomplice, Raul Mero, age 28, pleaded guilty earlier and testified against Hernandez in exchange for a lesser sentence. Hernandez faces the possibility of the death penalty. In her remarks to the jury, state's attorney Ann Ramos, who prosecuted the case, said Hernandez was part of a premeditated "kill team."

Prosecutors said Watson, a 25-year-old father of one, and his partner, Officer Wayne Smith, responded to a call in the 6000 block of South Huron Avenue just after midnight. Soon after exiting their vehicle, the two officers were fired upon and injured. According to testimony, Hernandez opened fire with a .357 Magnum while Mero fired a rifle. Mero testified that he wanted to leave, but Hernandez wanted to "finish the job" and shot Watson in the face at close range. Officer Smith, seriously injured, appeared to be dead, which saved his life.

In court Wednesday, Hernandez wore glasses, a blue scarf, and a white dress. Behind her, an unidentified relative sat with Hernandez's young daughter. "Don't be fooled by the look of motherly love, ladies and gentlemen," Ramos told jurors. "Life is about choices, and Miss Hernandez made the choice that night to kill in cold blood."

Hernandez will remain in Los Angeles County Jail pending her sentencing hearing. Prosecutors said they intend to ask for the death penalty despite

Hernandez's young age. "A community has lost a fine officer and a daughter has lost her father because of the cold, callous actions of Miss Hernandez," Ramos said. "She showed no mercy, so neither shall the state."

12

Camila saw him the second she walked into Mr. Bell's classroom for after-school math tutoring. Steven, leaning back in a chair, eyes on the door—on her.

She whirled around, sped out of the classroom and back down the empty hallway toward her locker. A moment later she heard footsteps behind her.

She made it to her locker just as Steven caught up to her.

"What's up, Killer Camila? I've been waiting for you."

He leaned toward her and rested both hands on her locker, one on either side of her head. His arms hemmed her in, his sly smile looming directly in front of her.

"Hey, back off!" Camila pushed him away, but his scrawny arms just shot back forward. As he leaned closer, his breath smelled foul, like rotted food.

"First we need to talk. I got a business proposal for you."

Camila felt sick. Here it was, the offer she'd always dreaded. A tattoo up the side of her arm, a gun in her hand, and her mother's future. "Not interested," she said.

"Look, you and me, we could have some fun, know what I'm saying?" Steven said.

"You got me wrong," Camila said. "I got a good thing here. I don't need to play your game. So why don't you just leave me alone?"

Steven laughed. An ugly laugh that echoed in the silent hall. "I hear you got some straight-laced A-student boyfriend, is that true?" He'd obviously been asking around about her.

"That's none of your business. *I'm* not your business."

More laughter. "Well, I'm gonna make you my business, Killer Camila. One way or another. Does he know about you? This perfect boyfriend? Does he know you like I do?"

She was cold all over, and at the same time she was sweating. "You leave him out of this."

"Uh-huh. That's what I thought. Tell you what, you can stick your nose up at me if you want, but just remember, all that good stuff you got going on here—I can make it go away. I can blow your precious little cover, Killer Camila. And then I won't be the only one who sees you for what you are."

Camila froze. She'd tried everything in the past when somebody found out. She became someone's best friend or worst enemy. She promised or threatened. Whatever it took to keep it quiet. It had to be kept quiet. Otherwise, as soon as people knew, even though she'd done nothing, in everyone's eyes she stood guilty.

"I don't want any trouble," Camila said, her voice breaking. She hated to show weakness, but it might be the only card she could play that would work. "Just let it go, please."

"OK." Steven put his hands on Camila's shoulders. "For a price."

"I don't have any—"

"Sure you do, girl. You got plenty I want." Steven turned his back and started to walk away. Camila stood, scared and confused, not sure what he meant, until Steven stopped in front of the boys' bathroom. With one hand, he opened the door. With the other he motioned for Camila to join him. Even from that distance, Camila saw the smirk filling Steven's face before he let the door swing shut behind him.

She'd done so much to protect her secret, to protect herself, to hide her shame. What was the price she'd pay?

Seeing no one in halls, she walked toward the bathroom. She got as far as the door, but the cold metal felt like it burned her flesh.

She turned and ran.

13

"Why did she do it?"

Aunt Maria looked up from her morning coffee in surprise. Camila sat down at the kitchen table beside her and waited.

She had always been scared to ask her mother this question, and the answer from every other family member had always been "drugs." But Camila was old enough to know that wasn't an answer. She just needed to look around the street corners of her neighborhood to see junkies and drunks. None of them ever killed anyone, let alone a police officer. And her mother hadn't just killed, she had murdered in cold blood.

"It was a long time ago," Aunt Maria said slowly, "and I was only a kid myself. But I know she and your grandmother didn't get along. The more our mother tried to control Gina, the worse it got. Then she got into drugs and the gang, or maybe the other way around. Gina left her family behind for gang life long before she went to prison. She was a selfish person, Camila, selfish and impulsive. She did what she did partly, I think, because she never thought about the consequences. For herself or for others. She didn't think about that police officer's life because she never thought about her own. She didn't think about his family for the same reason."

Camila nodded. *She* had thought about Officer Watson's family. About his wife, who had never stopped hating Gina Hernandez. About his daughter, a girl Camila's age. What would she feel in that girl's place? Was that girl's life easier in some ways, even though her father was gone? There must be some comfort,

Camila thought, in being the daughter of the victim instead of the murderer.

"But that doesn't mean she didn't love you," Aunt Maria added. "You would always light her up, Camila. I'm not saying that made her a better person or a better mother. She didn't do right by you—not by a long shot—but she's always loved you."

Camila stared at her hands, clasped together on the table. "Sometimes . . ." She swallowed. "Sometimes I just wish . . ." But there was no way to finish that sentence.

"You know, I really can't imagine what you've been through," Aunt Maria said, placing her hand gently on Camila's shoulder. "Not just growing up without your mom, but moving from place to place like you've done—paying for her crimes. I wish I knew how to make it easier."

Camila was at a loss for words. She'd given Maria so little credit over the past year—expecting this to be just another temporary stop on her odyssey from relative to relative. But Aunt Maria was trying. She cared, even though Camila had refused to open up to her.

"I don't want people to know," Camila confessed in a small voice. The voice of a scared seven-year-old. "I don't want them to think bad things."

"I understand. Believe me, I do," Aunt Maria said softly. "I had kids whose parents were police officers or guards. They would bully me, call me terrible names, push me around."

"Me too." Camila tried to block out the memory of seventh grade at Sierra. There had been a news story when the California Supreme Court wouldn't stay her mom's sentence. Camila wasn't mentioned by name, but some teacher made the connection and told someone else. By the end of the week, everybody knew. Lots of kids started calling her "Killer Camila." As bad as the name-calling was, it was nothing compared to the beating two girls, both of them cops' daughters, gave her one day in the playground. One girl punched Camila hard enough to break her own hand along with Camila's jaw.

She couldn't face it again.

"All I know is that for the longest time, she

wasn't sorry for what she did," Aunt Maria said. "In fact, she even seemed proud. But at least there's some small chance at salvation now that she's repented and asked for forgiveness."

"But the family of the—" Camila started but then stopped. She couldn't bring herself to say "the victim." That seemed like such a simple, empty word. "Officer Watson's family," she said.

Aunt Maria nodded. "Like I said the other day, they won't really heal until they forgive Gina."

"I don't think I could," Camila whispered. In a rush she added, "If I was his daughter, I mean. If it were the other way around, if someone had killed Mom—or you . . ." She trailed off and looked up at her aunt. "I don't think I could do it."

Aunt Maria nodded, staring into her coffee cup. "It's not an easy thing. But I think it's possible if you reach deep enough into your heart."

Camila felt like she was back at Sierra on the playground, except this punch hurt worse. They weren't talking about the Watsons anymore.

They were talking about what her mother had asked her to do, the last time they would ever speak to each other.

"Truth is, Aunt Maria, I don't know how I feel. Forty-nine percent of the time I love her because she's my mom. Forty-nine percent of the time I hate her because of what she did and how she's ruined so many lives, including mine."

"What about the other two percent?" Aunt Maria asked.

Camila looked not at her aunt, but up at the ceiling. "That's what keeps me up at night."

14

"So, what's it gonna be?" Steven asked. "You bailed on me before. Guess you needed time to think things over?"

Just like the last time they spoke, Steven was smirking. Though Camila had stayed away from Mr. Bell's after-school math tutoring, she knew she couldn't avoid Steven for the rest of the school year. She'd hoped to get through Friday, but he was in her face first thing this morning.

All around them lockers opened and closed, fingers clicked with furious texting, people sang under their headphones. The halls were filled with the energy of a new day starting. But yet again, Camila felt alone. Juan was already in a classroom somewhere, finishing up an early student government meeting. And there was no one else in the whole school who cared about her, who would notice that she was in trouble.

Camila set her shoulders the way she used to do before a fight. "The answer's no. I'm not joining Los Reyes, and I'm not doing *you* any favors."

"So I guess you don't mind going public about your mom, then."

"My mom's crimes aren't mine. Just let me alone."

"Like I said, if it was me, I'd be bragging about how my mom killed a cop, but that's—"

"That cop had a daughter," Camila said. "What about her? Did you think about that? What was it like for her to grow up without a dad? What was it like for me to grow up without a mother?"

Steven sniffed, like he didn't know what to say.

"Steven, I don't understand why you want to

hurt me," Camila said, almost begging.

"I don't want to hurt you, Camila," Steven said. "I just want—" An almost slithering arm came toward Camila.

Camila knocked his hand away. "Don't touch me."

"What are you going to do about it?"

Camila took Steven's left hand in her right and raised them both so they were shoulder high. She gently squeezed his hand, and for a half-second, her coy smile seemed like a real smile . . .

Until she jammed her knee hard between Steven's legs. Just as quickly she pulled her hand away and fixed it into the shape of pistol. She dug her index finger hard into Steven's forehead, the nail piercing the skin. A small trickle of blood fell into Steven's eyes, which were closed in pain, and then Camila spoke, her voice calm as a stone cold killer's.

"Guess I didn't make myself clear. You understand me now?"

Steven swallowed hard and nodded. He didn't open his eyes—probably because if he did, Camila would see the fear in them.

Camila turned and headed toward advisory. Behind her, she heard Steven mumble, "Like mother, like daughter."

She didn't turn back.

15

"Father Gomez, can I speak with you?" Camila had stayed late after youth group.

"Is something troubling you, Camila?"

"Yes—can we talk, in your office?" The confessional might be better suited, but going to confession had always freaked Camila out.

"Absolutely," said Father Gomez.

Camila followed him through the activity center and back into the church. Father Gomez directed Camila to a chair across from his overflowing desk.

"I wanted to apologize for the other week, you know, running out on the group," Camila started. All the way over on the bus, she'd thought about what to say, about how to begin.

"Nothing to worry about," Father Gomez said. "We all have our bad days."

"So I'm forgiven."

"Of course." He smiled, but his expression changed when he saw Camila's tears. "What's wrong?"

"Is it that easy? Is it that easy to forgive someone?" Camila asked.

"The Bible tells us that no matter how serious the sin, God is willing to forgive us. But walking out on youth group isn't a serious sin."

Camila couldn't look up.

"Camila," said Father Gomez softly, "is there something else you want to tell me?"

Camila drew a long, slow breath. "Yes, there is." Then she told Father Gomez about her mother, her crime, and her approaching execution. She talked so fast, the words fell over each other. Only once before had she told anyone. Back in fifth grade, she told her best friend, Gabriella Diaz. It felt good to tell someone, until they weren't best friends anymore. They'd gotten into a fight over something Camila no longer remembered. And Gabriella had told. After that, what little trust she had to give, she held inside, afraid to surrender it again. Until Juan, she'd avoided relationships for that very reason.

"Camila, I'm so sorry. I will pray for you and your mother. Has she repented?"

"She says she has." But Camila wondered if her mom meant it. Gina had lied for so long about so many things, like every time she signed a letter *Love*. If her mother loved her, she would be there for her, not two hundred miles away, trapped like an animal in a cage, waiting to die.

"But I don't know if I can forgive her. I love her, but I also hate her for causing all this pain."

"Forgiveness is the only way to heal that pain, the only way to peace," Father Gomez said.

"I just feel so all alone in the world," Camila confessed. While Father Gomez assured her she was not alone, Camila thought of her mother, soon to be strapped in a chair, as alone as a person could be. *Maybe God forgives, but the State of California doesn't.*

16

Aunt Rosa stormed into Aunt Maria's apartment before Camila had even finished opening the door for her.

"I've been calling for hours!" Aunt Rosa fumed as she bulldozed her way into the living room. *Nice to see you too*, Camila didn't bother to say.

"We didn't want to answer the phone," said Aunt Maria, coming out of the kitchen. "The press."

Camila doubted that was the real reason. She knew firsthand how difficult Rosa could be. Things hadn't ended well between them, and

Camila had avoided her ever since. Or maybe it was Aunt Rosa avoiding her. Either way, Camila was rarely happy to see her.

"You took the train?" Maria asked Rosa as Rosa dumped an overnight bag on the couch.

"Of course I took the train. And you weren't there to meet me at the station. Because you weren't answering the phone. I had to—"

"Are you hungry?" Aunt Maria talked over her older sister. "Dinner's almost ready."

Five minutes later the three of them were sitting at the table, eating in chilly silence.

"So what did she choose?" Aunt Rosa asked finally. "Lethal injection or electric chair?"

Camila's food lurched in her stomach. She set her fork down.

"Let's not talk about that," said Maria.

"Not talk about it? You think I came out here to *not* talk about it? To just ignore it?"

"You didn't have to come," Camila muttered.

Aunt Rosa glared at her. "Of course I had to come! The family should be together for something like this."

"Yeah, because you've always been so supportive and comforting," Camila retorted before she could stop herself.

"Don't talk to me that way, young lady. Show some respect. If you're not careful you're going to end up just like—"

"Rosa, don't start," Aunt Maria snapped. "Camila's not going to be like Gina."

Camila froze. It was the first time she'd ever heard Aunt Maria, or any relative, say those words.

"Anyway, you always talk about Gina like she was a monster," Aunt Maria went on. "She wasn't a monster. She was a scared and lost young woman who made a terrible mistake." Camila noticed that Maria was already talking about Gina in the past tense.

"You're too forgiving, Maria," Rosa shot back. "I was there. You were just a kid."

"Then tell me, Aunt Rosa, why did she do it?" Camila said quietly. "You're her older sister. You were there for all of it. You tell us."

Rosa struggled for an answer. "How can I know what was in another person's heart?"

"Exactly," said Camila. "We don't know. We'll probably never know. So what's the point of throwing blame around now? What's the point of building more walls?"

Her aunts both stared at her—one with surprise and suspicion, one with love and maybe even pride.

Camila picked up her fork again and went back to eating her dinner.

17

Camila hadn't slept all night. By the time she called Juan on Aunt Maria's landline, the darkness had started to turn gray.

"Hello?" Juan's voice on the other end was a heavy mumble.

"Juan, it's Camila," she whispered, praying her aunts wouldn't wake up. "I'm sorry, but I need to ask you a big favor."

"At four in the morning? What am I, a farmer?"

Camila knew he meant it as a joke, but she didn't laugh. "I need a ride."

"Where do you need to go?" Juan asked, now sounding just confused.

She hesitated. "The other day, Juan, you said you loved me," she said softly. "If that's true, that means I can trust you, right?"

"Of course, Camila."

"And that no matter what, you'll be there for me, right?"

"Yes."

"Good, then get over here as soon as you can. Gas up the car because it's a long drive."

***

By the time they reached Chowchilla, Camila had told Juan everything she'd told Father Gomez, and more. Not just about her mother, but about herself. The bullying at other schools, the shoplifting, her party days in Riverside, her night in juvenile hall. Everything except the incidents with Steven earlier in the week. All the time she talked, Juan said very little, asking hardly any questions. The more she talked, the more she needed to keep going. With each sentence she felt as if a weight had been lifted from her chest, as if she could finally breathe freely again.

"I'm sorry I didn't tell you before," she said at last. "It's just that trusting someone is—"

"It's OK, Camila. First of all, I don't blame you for what your mom did. And as for what you've done—that's your past. It doesn't have to be your future. I know you don't want it to be. And I know there's so much more to you. So much that I love."

Juan took his right hand off the wheel and reached out for Camila. She wrapped both of her hands around Juan's hand: hard knuckles, soft skin, her life, his life. "Thank you, Juan."

They were getting close to the prison now. "What time is the execution?" asked Juan.

"Midnight. In Folsom."

"Looks like we're not the only ones who showed up early."

He was right. Protestors had gathered all along the road. Some carried signs that seemed to celebrate her mom's approaching execution: *Kill the Cop Killer!* Others called for an end to the death penalty, like the one held by a girl about Camila's age—a white girl with long brown hair: *Mercy, Not Vengeance.* Trucks with logos from LA TV stations lined the side of the road, complete with dish antennas. Camila wanted to scream at them all to go away. This had nothing to do with them or their stupid causes. "Look at all this!" Juan breathed, almost in awe.

Camila didn't want to look at it. For a while, on the way here, she'd felt so hopeful. Juan had been so understanding, so accepting. She'd started to believe this could be easy after all. But that simple joy was gone now. Her heart was no calmer than the scene outside: noisy and complicated, filled with anger and hurt. Would that all go away once her mother was dead? Would Camila be able to snatch back that breath of freedom she'd felt during the drive here? Or had her mom gotten death while Camila got life without parole?

18

"How can you not let me see her?"

The gray-haired, white-faced warden remained unmoved. He'd been called when Camila, with Juan's support, refused to leave after being turned away by the gatekeeper guards. "You know the rules, Miss Hernandez. A minor needs to be with a legal guardian."

Camila pointed over the warden's shoulder. "My mother is in there!"

"Your mother is not your legal guardian, as I recall," the warden said. "Even if she was, you also know the visiting hours are Saturdays

73

and Sundays, so—"

"She won't be alive next Saturday or Sunday!"

The warden gently grabbed Camila's arm. "I'm sorry, but you need to go."

"I need to speak with her!" Camila yelled. "I need to say good-bye."

"You need to leave now. If you don't—"

Juan stepped forward. He put his hand on Camila's arm, just above the warden's hand. "We're not leaving."

The warden let go of Camila's arm as a look of surprise came over his face. Camila guessed he was not a person often defied. "I'm afraid there's no other option," he said.

Camila started to speak, her voice thick with tears, but Juan jumped in. "There are TV trucks outside. If you don't let Camila see her mother, then that's our next stop. Do you really want the entire world to know that you denied a daughter a chance to say good-bye to her loving mother?"

Camila could've kissed him right in front of the warden. *Thank you, Juan. Thank you for being here for me*. It had been so long since anyone had stood up for her. One of the consequences, maybe, of living most of her life alone.

The warden smirked. Just a tiny uptick of his lips. Easy to miss, if you hadn't seen it on a million other faces. "Her loving mother is a convicted murderer. And it's not my job to worry about what the press thinks. Miss Hernandez, I'm sorry, but if you don't leave now, I'll need to call the police."

"I just want to say good-bye and tell her that . . ." Camila started.

"You don't need to call the police," Juan said. "We'll leave. Let's go, Camila."

Juan wrapped his arms around Camila and turned her toward the exit. About halfway there, she broke free and raced back to the warden. "Call the chaplain."

"What?" the warden asked.

"Doesn't she see the chaplain before—"

"That's not normal procedure..."

"Call him, please," said Juan.

The warden said nothing for the longest time. Then: "Wait here, I'll see if I can I find her." He turned away, cell phone in hand.

Juan pulled Camila closer. She kissed him, but then her eyes scanned the familiar room. She broke away and went over to pick up a visitor application, along with a short yellow pencil. Sitting at the hard table, she turned the application over and started to write.

Dear Mother,

I came up here to see you, but they wouldn't let me in. Locked out again. All my life that's how I've felt. Locked out, not just from you, but everything. It was like life was happening for everybody else, and I could see it, but I couldn't be part of it. I was left alone. And I've kept people away, afraid they would find out about you and think that I was like you. I've even kept you away, more than the prison's bars and guards ever did. I was afraid to trust anyone. Including you. Including myself.

But that's not why I'm writing this letter for the chaplain to give to you.

I know that Officer Watson's family can't forgive you. But I do.

I forgive you, Mother. Not for what you did,

because that has nothing to do with me, and it's not my place. I don't know why you did what you did, but I don't need to know. The important thing is that I forgive you for what you couldn't do: be there to be my real mother. To raise me. To love me.

You're still part of me. And I'm done being ashamed of that.

I love you. I forgive you. I miss you, but then again, I always have. And I always will.

Love,

Camila

19

Camila was so tired every part of her body ached. But she knew she couldn't go to bed. Instead she sat on the couch with Aunt Rosa and Aunt Maria, drinking coffee and watching the news. She hadn't mentioned her prison visit this morning. Juan had gotten them back to Anaheim well before school let out, and they'd spent a few hours at his favorite coffee shop before she'd gone home at her usual time. Both aunts had assumed she'd been at school. She hadn't had to lie. She was done lying. If it ever came up, she'd be honest about what had happened today.

"It's a circus," said Rosa, which was the first understatement Camila had ever heard her aunt make.

The cameras were stationed outside Folsom Prison now. And the protesters seemed to have moved with them. There were more people now than there'd been at the women's facility this morning. An equal number on each side. The TV reporter, a pretty young black woman, struggled to shout over the noise surrounding her.

"This marks the first execution of a woman in two years, and the first in California..." Camila couldn't mute the TV, so she just stopped listening. Her mom wasn't a story or a statistic. This wasn't a cause or a reason for celebration.

Suddenly the reporter's voice caught her attention again. "... I'm speaking with Sophie Watson, the seventeen-year-old daughter of..."

"Turn it up!" Camila gasped, leaning forward. Aunt Rosa picked up the remote and raised the volume a few notches.

Standing next to the reporter was a girl Camila recognized. It was the girl with long brown hair who'd been at Gina's prison this morning. In her hand was a sign. It was now turned sideways, but Camila read it easily since she remembered the words: *Mercy, Not Vengeance*.

"I won't be consumed by bitterness and hatred," Sophie Watson said, her voice shaking with emotion. "My mother has never forgiven Gina Hernandez, but I've accepted my loss. The only thing to do is to replace the loss with something else. I can choose love and forgiveness over hate and bitterness. That's how I've found peace."

Camila looked away from the TV to glance at her aunts. Through the tears that blurred her eyes, she saw Rosa put a hand on Aunt Maria's arm. Camila leaned over and wrapped her arms around Maria. Her aunt hugged her back. The reporter's words faded, drowned out by the sobs of Gina Hernandez's family.

20

People knew. Camila sensed it the moment she walked into advisory.

"Why didn't you tell us?" Lisa, with Angela, behind her, was the first to say anything.

"Tell you what?" Old habits died hard. Most things died hard, really.

"About your mom," Lisa whispered.

"I'm so sorry for your loss," said Angela.

Camila felt words jam up in her throat. She had no idea what to say, and even less idea what to feel.

"I lost my mom a few years ago to breast

81

cancer," Lisa said. "It's hard."

"For me, it's my dad," Angela added. "He's alive, but not really part of the family. He's been in and out prison most of my life. I see him every now and then, but it's not the same."

"I'm sorry, Angela," Camila finally said.

"It's not my fault, so you don't need to feel sorry for me, but I appreciate it anyway," Angela said. "Look, everybody's parents make mistakes. Some get caught, and some don't. We don't judge."

"How'd you find out about my mom?" Camila asked. "Did Steven tell you?"

"Who's Steven?" said Lisa. Angela shrugged.

"Then how do you know?" Even as she asked, she prayed the answer wouldn't be Juan.

"I don't remember how it started, I think from somebody at Corona High who knew somebody who goes here, but this got sent around." Lisa showed Camila her phone. It was a screen capture of Gina's old yearbook photo, the one they'd shown on TV, next to a photo of Camila from last year's Corona High yearbook. "You look a lot like your mom."

"I know, but I'm nothing like her."

"We wouldn't know about that," Lisa said. Camila's eyes flashed in anger, and she stepped away. "Sorry, I didn't mean anything bad."

"She means we wouldn't know that because we don't know anything about you," Angela said. "I mean, Camila, do you even have any friends?"

Camila didn't answer the question. "Friends betray you."

"Well, that's the chance you take," Lisa replied. "But you know, I'd rather take that chance then never be able to trust anyone. I mean that must be terrible. You must feel—"

"All alone in the world," Camila said.

"I felt like that too sometimes," Angela said. "First time my dad got locked up."

There was genuine concern and caring in their voices. Camila wondered if she'd made a mistake—trying so hard to protect her secret that she had surrendered a good part of life. Maybe trust was like forgiveness. It had to be given freely. And freely received.

"We're going to the mall later. Do you want

to come with?" Lisa asked.

"Why, you need a necklace you want me to steal?" Camila snapped back.

"No, we just thought you'd like the company," Lisa answered. "I know after my mom died, I just wanted to be left alone, but I realize now that was the worst thing in the world."

Camila held in her tears and nodded. *OK, I'll give it a try. I'll give them—and myself—a fair chance.* She allowed herself to smile at the thought of finally unlocking her life.

AFTERWORD

As of 2014, it's estimated that more than 2.7 million children in the United States have a parent behind bars. About one in five of those kids are teenagers. While having parents in prison presents challenges at any age, it may be particularly hard for teenagers, as they try to find their way in the world.

The *Locked Out* series explores the realities of parental incarceration through the eyes of teens dealing with it. These stories are fictional, but the experiences that Patrick Jones writes about are daily life for many youths.

The characters deal with racism, stigma, shame, sadness, confusion, and isolation—common struggles for children with parents in prison. Many teens are forced to move from their homes, schools, or communities as their families cope with their parents' incarcerations.

These extra challenges can affect teens with incarcerated parents in different ways. Kids often struggle in school – they are at increased risk for skipping school, feeling disconnected from classmates, and failing classes. They act out and test boundaries. And they're prone to taking risks, like using substances or engaging in other illegal activities.

In addition, studies have shown that youth who are involved in the juvenile justice system are far more likely than their peers to have a parent in the criminal justice system. In Minnesota, for example, boys in juvenile correctional facilities are ten times more likely than boys in public schools to have a parent currently incarcerated. This cycle of incarceration is likely caused by many factors. These include systemic differences in the distribution of wealth and resources, as well as bias within policies and practices.

The *Locked Out* series offers a glimpse into this complex world. While the books don't sugarcoat reality, each story offers a window of hope. The teen characters have a chance to thrive despite difficult circumstances. These books highlight the positive forces that make a difference in teens' lives: a loving, consistent caregiver; other supportive, trustworthy adults; meaningful connections at school; and participation in sports or other community programs. Indeed, these are the factors in teens' lives that mentoring programs around the country aim to strengthen, along with federal initiatives such as My Brother's Keeper, launched by President Obama.

This series serves as a reminder that just because a parent is locked up, it doesn't mean kids need to be locked out.

—Dr. Rebecca Shlafer
Department of Pediatrics,
University of Minnesota

AUTHOR ACKNOWLEDGMENTS

Thanks to Dr. Rebecca J. Shlafer and members of her research team for reading and commenting on this manuscript. Also thanks to Madison from South St Paul Community Learning Center for her manuscript review.

ABOUT THE AUTHOR

Patrick Jones is the author of more than twenty-five novels for teens. He has also written two nonfiction books about combat sports: *The Main Event*, on professional wrestling, and *Ultimate Fighting*, on mixed martial arts. He has spoken to students at more than one hundred alternative schools and has worked with incarcerated teens and adults for more than a decade. Find him on the web at www.connectingya.com and on Twitter: @PatrickJonesYA.

RETURNING TO NORMAL

PATRICK JONES

TAKING SIDES

PATRICK JONES

GUARDING SECRETS

PATRICK JONES

RAISING HEAVEN

PATRICK JONES

DOING RIGHT

PATRICK JONES

CHECK OUT ALL OF THE TITLES IN THE LOCKED OUT SERIES